$7.95

90-58

DATE DUE

CRITTERLAND ADVENTURES

The Critter Race

Story and pictures by Bob Reese

 CHILDRENS PRESS, CHICAGO

MY 30 WORDS ARE:

all	their	slow
the	place	whoa
critter	nice	here
like	mean	there
to	black	everywhere
run	green	it
have	has	was
fun	begun	just
race	fast	done
take	and	for

Library of Congress Cataloging in Publication Data
Reese, Bob.
  The critter race.

  (Critterland adventures)
  Summary: The desert animals have a race for fun.
  [1. Desert animals—Fiction.   2.   Racing—Fiction.
3.   Stories in rhyme]   I.   Title.   II.   Series.
PZ8.3.R255Cr   [E]   81-3874
ISBN 0-516-02302-0   AACR2

TWEEDLE-DE-DEE
HILL
THE
SANDY
SAND
LACTUS
CACTUS
HUZZARD
BUZZARD
TREE
SCARY
LARRY
LAND
GRASSHOPPER TRAIL
DRY
WASH
GRASSHOPPER
LAND
ROADRUNNER
ROCK
CLIFFS

All the critters

like to run.

All the critters

like having fun.

Critters like

to critter race.

All the critters

take their place.

Nice critters,

mean critters,

13

Black critters,

green critters.

Run, run, run.
Fun, fun, fun.

The critter race
has just begun.

Nice and mean,
black and green.

Fast and slow.
Whoooa!!!

Critters here.
Critters there.

Critters, critters
everywhere!

It was nice.
The race was done.

The critter race
was all for fun.

Bob Reese was born in 1938 in Hollywood, California. His mother Isabelle was an English teacher in the Los Angeles City Schools.

After his graduation from high school he went to work for Walt Disney Studios as an animation cartoonist. He received his B.S. degree in Art and Business and began work as a freelance illustrator and designer.

He currently resides in the mountains of Utah with his wife Nancy and daughters Natalie and Brittany.